PRESENTED BY

Hart Law

BALDER
and the
MISTLETOE

BALDER
and the
MISTLETOE

*A Story for
the Winter Holidays*

◆

retold by EDNA BARTH

pictures by RICHARD CUFFARI

◆

Houghton Mifflin/Clarion Books/New York

Second printing

Text copyright © 1979 by Edna Barth
Illustrations copyright © 1979 by Richard Cuffari

Printed in the United States of America

Library of Congress Cataloging in Publication Data
    Barth, Edna.   Balder and the mistletoe.
    SUMMARY: A retelling of the Norse legend of how
    Balder, god of light and joy, was brought down by the
    evil Loki with an arrow made of mistletoe.
      1.   Balder—Juvenile literature.   2.   Loki—Juvenile
literature.   [1.   Balder.   2.   Loki.   3.   Mythology,
    Norse]   I.   Cuffari, Richard, 1925—   II.   Title.
  PZ8.1.B3Bal   [398.2]   78-4523   ISBN 0-395-28956-4

To George

Balder the Bright, a god of light and joy, was best loved of the Aesir, as the gods and goddesses of the North were once called.

In Asgard, home of the Aesir, Balder lived within the Peacestead. There no foul or false word was ever spoken, no blood ever shed, and no crime ever committed. There truth, purity, and harmony prevailed.

Balder himself was fairest of all the gods, with hair as bright as sunlight and eyes as blue as the northern skies. And though he was of high rank, being a son of Odin, oldest of the gods, his bearing was free of any arrogance. Wherever Balder walked, he radiated peace and well-being, and so was beloved by all. Every white flower was named for Balder, and every bird of the air sang his praises.

No darkness had ever touched Balder. But what is fated must come to pass, and one morn-

ing Balder sprang from his couch, awakened by dreams of his own death.

Death—a plunge into cold and darkness! To one who had lived in radiance, the notion was past imagining. His brow tightened by a frown, Balder paced the shining halls of his castle, recalling his dream.

He had seen, in sharp outline, the hull of his ship *Ringhorn* and the flame and smoke of his own funeral pyre. And he had seen his father Odin, King of Heaven, his mother, Queen Frigga, and the rest of the Aesir, weeping for him.

With the vision of his own end had come a glimpse of the world stripped of all greenery. This fragment of the dream had been so faint and fleeting that Balder could barely recall it.

That morning he stayed within his castle, silent and brooding. How could he break the news to his wife, the gentle and loving Nanna? How could he tell the rest of the Aesir? For it was no secret to Balder that he was their favorite. "I must spare them," he decided. "The dream must be kept secret." With that, his heart lightened a little, for Balder was more given to soothing and healing than to causing pain.

Before long, though, the gloom returned. Balder's windows looked out on a landscape golden with sunlight, but he saw it as if in shadow. The warm breeze stealing softly into the room seemed to whisper of cold and harshness.

Nanna, aware of Balder's mood, grew frightened. Never before had she seen his face darkened by a frown or his eyes without their glow. A chill entered her heart, and she dared not speak to Balder. The servants exchanged troubled glances and kept their distance.

Balder himself remained aloof, struggling with his terrible secret. Finally, he could bear it no longer, so, leaving the Peacestead, he mounted his horse Lightfoot and rode to Valhalla, the timbered hall of his father Odin.

Balder's coming was well-timed. Odin had just dispatched his aides, the mighty Valkyrie, to the world's battlefields. There they would select those warriors who were to fall and would transport them to Valhalla, hall of heroes. Balder could see them—Hilda, Mista, and the others—galloping off on their white chargers through the upper air. Even though it was daytime, the lights from their armor made a many-colored flashing in the northern skies.

The spirits of slain warriors who feasted each evening with Odin had gone out to battle in the vast courtyard, as they did each day. Hugin and

Munin, Odin's pet ravens, were off on their daily news-gathering flight through all the worlds. Except for his pet wolves and a few servants, Odin sat alone in his hall of 640 doors.

The moment Balder appeared before him, Odin saw that something of grave import had happened. When the younger god asked for a gathering of the Aesir, Odin quickly agreed. "Down with you!" he said sternly to a jealous wolf cub who leapt at Balder.

Word was sent forth, and the Aesir soon
gathered, alarmed at the new Balder they saw
before them.

Balder scanned the faces. He saw Bragi,

14

foremost of poets and teller of never-ending tales in which Balder had once delighted. Nearby stood the shapely Freya, whose concern was beauty and ripeness in living things. Thor, wielder of thunderbolts, had come holding his famous hammer, his blue eyes fierce and vengeful, his gross appetite for meat and drink held in check out of love for Balder.

Watching with anxious eyes was Balder's mother, the stately Frigga, protector of marriage. Close beside her, pale as the white robe she wore, was Balder's wife, Nanna, with their son, the tall Forseti, settler of disputes and lawsuits.

So beloved was Balder that all the Aesir were there—except Heimdall, the Watchman. For the Rainbow Bridge of Bifrost, the entrance to Asgard, must be guarded at all times. Otherwise, the Aesir's enemies, the Frost Giants and all the monsters and demons of the worlds, would swarm in and take possession.

At a nod from Odin, Balder arose, unable to

speak at first. Finally he announced, "I have dreamed of my own death!"

A chill spread through the vast hall. Balder's presence among the Aesir was like the warmth and beauty of summer; the Peacestead in which he lived, a haven in which the Aesir found strength and joy. Without this, they would long since have surrendered to gloom as they thought of the powerful forces arrayed against them.

"I have dreamed of my own death!" Balder's words reached the walls and came echoing back.

The Aesir's cries of outrage rang out over all the worlds. Winds and breezes stopped blowing, tides halted, birds poised in their flight.

* * *

In Odin the shock went deepest, for he felt his own power weaken and had a vision of the final battle of gods and Frost Giants. Odin strode from the hall to his watchtower, there to await Hugin and Munin, his ravens.

Before long, two black specks against the vast blue of the heavens signaled their return. Soon, there was a whirring, then a flapping, and the two ravens hurtled down onto Odin's shoulders.

"What have you learned today?" demanded Odin, stern and distant.

"This day we have learned what is going on in the underworld," the ravens replied. There, in the hall of Hela, ruler of the dead, they reported, a couch had been spread, mead had been brewed, and a bench strewn with gold for some-one of high rank.

"And who might that be?" asked Odin with a strange laugh that startled the ravens.

They knew not, they said, with an anxious ruffle of their black wings. What they did know they had learned at the World Tree. Ratatosk the squirrel had heard it from the serpent who gnaws constantly at the roots. The squirrel, in turn, had told the news to the great eagle who roosts at the top, the same eagle whose wing-flapping causes gusts of wind in the world of mortals. The eagle had passed it on to Odin's ravens.

"We know not for whom Hela has done these things," Hugin and Munin repeated, neither one looking Odin in the eye.

* * *

The rest of the Aesir were giving voice to their shock and fear. "By what means will Balder die?" they wondered.

"Surely none in Asgard, or anywhere in the worlds, would want to *kill* Balder," said Frigga.

"None anywhere would want to kill him," echoed the others, in tones that belied their words. For not one of them, even Balder, lacked for enemies.

"Balder . . . ." The tall, gray-eyed Iduna arose, she who guarded the apples of youth so dear to the Aesir. "Balder"— Iduna faltered— "did your dream show how you are fated to end your life? If we knew this, it might be that we could help."

"The dream foretold only that my end is near," Balder replied, shuddering at the recollection.

Then the Aesir discussed the many ways in which their favorite might meet his end.

"From the sting of a poisonous serpent," suggested Bragi, flinching.

"Gored by a beast of the forest," said Balder's son Forseti, paling at the thought.

"From the blow of a powerful hammer," said Thor in a tone that made the rest of the Aesir tremble.

Frigga's eyes filled with such horror that none could look upon her. Then the goddess Eir, physician to the Aesir, suggested, "Balder could die of some dread disease. We must consider that, Frigga."

"He might drown in water," put in another goddess.

"Or be consumed by fire," said still another.

The gods and goddesses considered every form that death can take. If they could find out how Balder was to be destroyed, they could prevent it, or so they reasoned.

"But how can we find out?" demanded Frigga, her voice rising. "Balder has told you! His dream gave no clue!"

"True, true," murmured Bragi the thoughtful, his eyes cast downward. "We might protect Balder from deadly weapons only to have him killed by some ferocious beast. We might protect him from water and lose him to fire." Bragi looked up. "There is only one way. We must protect Balder, not from one danger or another, but from *every* danger."

"Yes, yes!" called out the others. Then they discussed how this would be brought about.

Frigga, it was decided, would visit everything in heaven and on earth, things that lived and breathed and things that did not. From each she would exact a promise not to harm Balder.

"With that done," said Frigga, "we shall be at ease, knowing that Balder will continue to smile upon us." Frigga smiled herself.

Cheered by the Aesir's plan, Balder retired to

his castle with a group of companions. The other gods and goddesses went off about their usual duties and pleasures—all but Frigga.

* * *

Frigga's chariot, with its drapings of rich fabrics, was made ready, but she sent it away, choosing instead to ride off on Fast Galloper, her swiftest horse.

Frigga visited earth, air, fire, and water. And each one, after hearing her story, vowed never to harm Balder. Next, Frigga went to stone, iron, and other metals. These, too, pledged to spare Balder.

Then Frigga spoke to every bird of the air, to every beast of the field and forest, to every lizard, snake, and crawling creature, as well as to every fish and every insect. No creature that flew, walked, crawled, or crept, swam, or fluttered, was forgotten. Nor did Frigga overlook any sickness or foul disease that might harm Balder.

Last of all, Frigga called on every shrub and vine, every tree, flower, and weed, and from each one she came away with the same promise.

Satisfied with her work, Frigga traveled wearily homeward. Just east of Valhalla, she noticed one little plant that she had overlooked. Its name was mistletoe. An odd little evergreen, with pearly, white berries, the mistletoe was growing on the branch of an old oak tree.

Frigga reined in her horse, meaning to exact the same oath from the mistletoe that she had from thousands of other plants. In her weariness, she looked at the tiny plant with no roots in the earth, clinging for its life to the branch of the ancient oak.

"Poor, puny little thing," said Frigga, "what harm could you do to one as strong and robust as Balder?"

The humble mistletoe lacked even the courage to answer. So Frigga dismissed the idea of demanding a promise from such an unimportant little parasite. Instead she rode on, her task completed, or so she believed.

With Frigga's return, the gloom that had fallen over the Aesir lifted. Balder himself, his mind serene again, walked in his former radiance.

Reveling in the safety of their favorite and wishing to celebrate, the gods devised a game. Standing Balder in their midst, they made a target of him. "Thanks to Frigga, nothing on heaven or earth can do you injury," they gloated, "and we shall prove this."

Bringing darts and arrows, swords and spears, axes, clubs, and boulders, the gods took their

aim. Some shot at Balder, some hewed at him, while others pelted him with rocks or hurled clubs at him. And when every weapon, even the deadliest, glanced off his shining form, the gods exulted.

After that, whenever they gathered, the gods enjoyed this sport, and Balder was honored.

Then one day, there appeared among them an onlooker who was and was not a member of the Aesir. His name was Loki. Though the son of a Jotun or Frost Giant, Loki was not ugly and monstrous, but handsome and fine-mannered. He was no more to be trusted than any Frost Giant however, and he often took shapes other than his own in order to confuse and deceive the Aesir.

Loki's polished manner had once fooled even Odin. That was long ago, of course, before Odin had acquired wisdom from the spring at the roots of the World Tree, giving one of his eyes for it. Loki had tricked Odin into adopting him as a blood brother. Thus he was free to come and go among the Aesir.

Watching the gods at their game, Loki was astonished. All around him were flashing spears, swords and javelins, swinging axes, and humming bowstrings. Yet, all this left Balder quite unharmed. At the feet of the smiling god were piled the powerless weapons, the mound growing ever higher as Loki watched.

Loki's face darkened with hatred. What special power was protecting this figure of light and joy? Loki would have asked, but he was choking with rage. Besides, he was well aware that the gods distrusted him. So slipping away, Loki took the shape of an old woman and hurried off to Frigga's dwelling, Fensalir, Hall of Mists.

There, Frigga sat at her wheel in deep content, spinning golden thread. Still rejoicing over Balder's safety, she was unsuspecting and full of trust. When told that an old woman had come to the door with something to tell her, she said lightly, "Let the old one come in."

The bent creature who entered bore no likeness to anyone Frigga knew. "There is something you ought to know," she said in a false quaver. "Your son Balder is in danger."

Even as the old woman spoke, the gleeful shouts of the gods could be heard in the distance. She went on to describe how the gods were trying to strike Balder down, while Balder did nothing but smile. "I fear your son has lost his wits," finished the old woman.

Frigga's face, which at first had looked troubled, quickly cleared. "Oh," she said with relief, "be assured that my son is in no danger. By pitting their weapons against Balder, the other gods are paying honor to him. No weapon in the

world can injure Balder—I have seen to that. And what is more," Frigga confided, "Balder is safe from all other dangers, too. I myself went to earth, air, fire, and water, and each vowed not to harm my son.

"I went to every bird, beast and fish, every snake, lizard, and crawling creature, and every insect, too. None of these will harm Balder, for each gave me a solemn promise. No sickness or disease can harm him either."

The old woman's eyes widened for an instant. "Think of that!" she said. "With such a mother, there is no question of Balder's safety."

"And that's not all," said Frigga, pleased with the compliment. "Every shrub, vine, and tree made a promise, too, as did every flower, grass, and weed . . . every plant there is."

As she said this, the faintest shadow passed over Frigga's face, and the old woman who was Loki saw it. "*Every* plant?" she asked in pretended admiration.

Frigga frowned. The old one was becoming tiresome. "We might as well say *every* plant," she said sharply, rising to show the woman it was time for her to leave. "The only plant I ignored was a little thing known as mistletoe. Without the oak tree to which it clings, it would not even be alive. So, of course, I wasted no time on that."

"Of course not," agreed the old woman. "For how could anything so weak and frail do harm to Balder?" And away she hobbled, out of the palace.

Though she could not say why, Frigga felt no more ease that day. But Loki was filled with glee. Once out of Frigga's presence, he tore off his woman's clothes, took his own shape again, and hurried away.

In an oak thicket east of Valhalla, making sure he was unnoticed, Loki cut a sprig of mistletoe from the gnarled branch of an ancient oak. "Modest enough to look at," he thought, as he whittled the stem into a sharp point, "but deadly, as we shall see." Then feverish with excitement, he rushed to the clearing where the gods were still at play.

"Balder will live forever! Nothing can harm Balder!" Leaping about, the gods were laughing and shouting with joy. Each time a weapon glanced off Balder's shining form, a new shout rang out.

Loki looked on, sick with hatred. This favorite of the gods stood for all he detested most. He fingered the bit of mistletoe but postponed the moment of throwing, the better to savor it. His eyes swept from face to face. He saw Tyr, Bragi, Hjord and Freyr, as well as Thor, wielder of the hammer, and Ull, expert among archers. Standing by himself, outside the lively circle, stood Balder's blind half-brother, Hoder.

Loki studied him, his mind busy. Then slyly, he made his way to Hoder. Changing his voice to keep the blind god from knowing him, he asked, "Why are you not aiming weapons at Balder like the others?"

"I have nothing to throw," said Hoder morosely. "And little good it would do me if I had. I cannot see where Balder stands, for I am blind."

Loki murmured, as if in sympathy. "Take this," he said softly, slipping the mistletoe dart between Hoder's fingers. "I will guide your hand. It is only fair since all the others have the advantage in their good eyesight."

Pausing only for an instant, Loki took one last baleful look at Balder who, as always, was clad in a white tunic with gold armbands and had no breastplate, shield, or armor. Then lifting Hoder's hand, Loki drew it back and took aim.

The bit of mistletoe sped to its destination. And like a fir tree felled by Thor's lightning, Balder slowly toppled forward, dead before his shining body struck the ground.

Mute with shock, the Aesir stared at the life-

less form. The sky paled, and a shadow deep
and dense as night spread over all the worlds.

Frigga and her attendant Fulla came running,
their eyes large with horror at what they saw.
Then Frigga discovered the sprig of mistletoe
and knew how her son had come to die.

"But by whose hand?" Her eyes wild with
grief and anger, she looked around her at all the

faces, her gaze coming at last to Hoder's.

And sightless though he was, Hoder knew it. "By my hand!" he confessed with an expression of horror. Then, his voice breaking, he told of the deceitful stranger who had seemed to befriend him, giving him the tiny weapon and guiding his hand.

When Frigga heard this, there flashed before her a memory of the old woman who had tricked her into naming the one plant that had made no promise not to harm Balder. "Loki!" she cried.

The other gods and goddesses crowded around, and even those who had never been known to weep before wept with Frigga.

They looked for Loki but it did no good. Once he had worked his evil, he had changed his shape to that of a falcon and flown away.

* * *

For three days and nights the Aesir mourned for Balder, and each one in turn tried to bring him back to life.

Thor, donning his belt of strength, tried to revive Balder by force. Freyr caused a bracing rain to fall upon him. Freya played music designed to restore Balder's soul. Nanna cradled Balder's head in her arms while Iduna pressed golden juice from the apples of youth between his lips. Frigga flooded his lifeless body with warm tears.

Each god used his special powers, as did each goddess, but to no avail. And now the wailing that arose was like the wailing of winds at night in the dead of winter.

In the midst of the lamentations Odin appeared, most sorrowful of all, for he alone knew the full meaning of Balder's death. He bent over his son's body for some time. Looking up at last, he turned to Frigga. "Hela has robbed us."

"No! No! I will not have it!" Frigga rose to her full stature. "Hela may rule the world of the dead, but I am queen of the upper regions, and Balder belongs here."

Then passing among the Aesir, she asked,

"Which of you would like to win my favor? I have a plan for bringing Balder back to Asgard, but I need your help."

The faces of the Aesir brightened, then grew somber again as Frigga went on. She wanted one who would venture deep into the cold, dark regions of Hela's realm to offer a ransom for Balder's return.

At last, Hermod the Bold stepped forward. Hermod often served as messenger for the Aesir, but this errand would be more urgent than any other he had undertaken.

"His steed shall be Sleipnir," decreed Odin.

So Odin's eight-footed stallion was led forth, neighing with pleasure. Stroking the long silvery mane, Odin whispered in the horse's ear.

Then Hermod mounted and galloped off.

* * *

To those who remained in Asgard there fell the sad duties of Balder's funeral. First his body was covered with rich robes and gold

adornments befitting his rank. Then, one by one, the Aesir took leave of their favorite, each placing beside him a treasured possession.

The farewells over, Balder's body was carried to the shore, to his longship, the splendid *Ringhorn*.

Odin, his face like stone, gave orders for the launching, and all the strongest gods put their shoulders to the sorrowful task. The *Ringhorn's* timbers creaked and groaned, but, as if unable to face this duty, the great ship refused to move.

Again and again, the gods pooled their might, but to no avail.

"Summon Hyrrokin," said Odin at last.

This female giant, famous for her strength, launched the *Ringhorn* with such force that the worlds trembled. Sparks flew from beneath the hull, the rollers burst into flame, the sky brightened with a strange light.

When the waters calmed, Balder's body was carried aboard the ship. The pyre was ready, with dry kindling, branches, and logs. As a last gift, Odin placed on the pyre one of the greatest treasures of the Aesir, the ring of Draupnir.

Nanna, seeing Balder's pyre ready for burning, could bear no more. Her heart burst with sorrow, and her body was placed beside Balder's.

From the shore, the Aesir watched as the flames rose. In their light, Odin could be seen with his mouth close to Balder's ear, but what he whispered no one knew.

Then Odin came ashore, and the longship was borne away on the ebbing tide.

Balder was dead, and all warmth, peace, and well-being had died with him. So it seemed to the Aesir. They felt as mortals often do in cool climates at the end of summer.

* * *

All this time, Hermod the Bold had been riding the long dark road to Hela's kingdom. For nine days and nights he rode through rugged glens, each deeper and darker than the one before. Even the huge white head of his steed was invisible to him, so dense was the darkness. And he was chilled to the marrow with cold and dampness.

Still, Hermod rode on, and at last he came to the bridge spanning the great abyss between life and death. When the bridge shook under Sleipnir's hoofbeats, the keeper, a pale giant maiden, appeared.

"Who are you," she demanded, "whose face lacks the color of death?"

Hermod reined in his steed and gave his name to the giant maid.

"Only yesterday," she said, "five bands of dead men rode over this bridge, but the noise of the hoofbeats were as nothing compared to his." She eyed the eight-footed steed and gave a quick nod of recognition.

"Was Balder among those dead men," asked Hermod, "or has he passed this way?"

"He has crossed this bridge," the giant told him, "but if you wish to find him, you must journey to the hall of Hela. Take the road to the North."

Hermod thanked her and rode on, at last coming to the gates of Hel. There, without waiting to be admitted, he dug in his spurs. Sleipnir flew

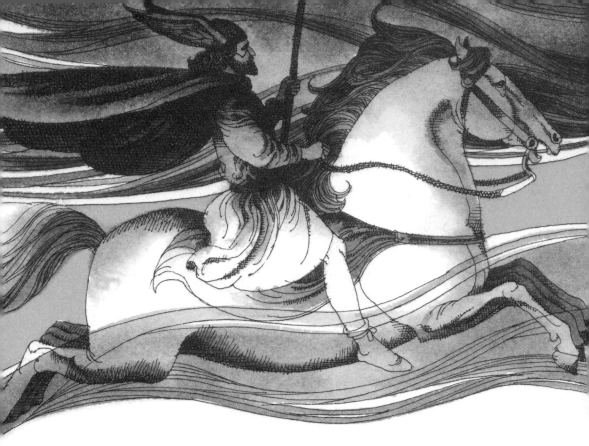

into the air, cleared the gates, and galloped northward.

Hermod rode on, the gloom growing always heavier and the dampness colder. All around him was a vast silence, broken only by the thud of Sleipnir's hoof beats.

At last, after many weary miles, Hermod saw, looming faintly before him, the spectral abode

of Hela. From within came a sighing and moaning of such hopelessness that Hermod was nearly overcome by it. He was tempted to leave this land of the dead before his own spirit completely drained from him.

But he forced his mind to the errand that had brought him here and, summoning all his will, dismounted and strode up to the gloomy portals.

A moment more and he was inside the dank hall of the fearful Hela, face to face with the queen herself. Clad in an ashen shroud, Hela sat in her high seat, her face cold and still as marble, looking straight before her out of eyes set in deep hollows.

Standing at her feet, Hermod felt a deathlike chill reach nearly to his heart. Then he saw, sitting next to Hela, Balder and Nanna. They both wore the dreadful pallor, but, lifeless though they appeared, their eyes brightened at the sight of Hermod.

As yet no one of the three spoke. Behind them, ghostly forms moved restlessly about among pillars turned green and mossy in the dampness of this place.

Finding his voice at last, Hermod paid his respects to Hela. "I have come," he explained, "with a message from Frigga, and while I am here, with your consent, I will have a word with Balder."

A frigid nod was Hela's only answer, but she ordered a basin, water, and towels for the traveler. His business would wait until he had bathed and rested, for this was the custom.

Rest held no interest for Hermod. All through the night he, Balder, and Nanna sat in a damp, unlighted chamber and talked, but what they spoke of no one knows.

Toward morning—what morning there is in that gloomy realm—Hermod sought out Hela and spoke of his errand. "I am here with an offer of ransom for Balder's return," he told her. "With those hordes of dead, why must you have

Balder?" The ghostly forms made a shifting pattern all around them as Hermod spoke.

Hela remained silent, her face empty of all feeling.

Then Hermod described what life was like without Balder. "There is nothing but sorrow and weeping," he said. "No eye remains dry."

"You say that all things in the worlds are weeping for Balder?" Hela asked.

"All things," said Hermod. "Those that live and breathe and those that do not."

"If this is really so," Hela announced, "then Balder may leave my kingdom, but I must have proof. If there is even one who refuses to weep, then Balder must remain here."

As Hermod prepared to leave, Balder led him aside. "Take this to Odin," he said, giving Hermod the ring Draupnir. Nanna gave Hermod fine linen for a headdress for Frigga.

Hermod rode joyfully back to Asgard, delivered the gifts, and related all he had seen and heard. "You have only to see that all things in the worlds weep for Balder," he finished, "all things, whether large or small."

The Aesir heard this with joy, but a joy that was mixed with caution. Had they not thought Balder safe before, only to have him killed by the lowly mistletoe? Soberly they repeated, "If all things large and small weep for Balder, he will return to us."

Thereupon messengers were dispatched throughout the worlds, and everything wept. Not only gods, goddesses, and mortals. Birds, beasts, fish, trees wept, and even stones and metals—as these things weep when brought out of the cold or frost into warmth.

Tears fell like rain, and the messengers turned homeward. As they approached Asgard, they noticed one crow who was not weeping. When they drew near, the crow flew away, cawing angrily. The messengers followed the bird through the forest to the entrance of a cave.

Suddenly, where the bird had been was a dry-eyed old woman.

"Who are you?" asked the messengers. "And why are you not helping to weep Balder out of Hel?"

"I am Thok," said the old woman, "and why should I weep for Balder? He's of no use to me, dead or alive." She gave a cruel laugh. "Let Hela have him."

The messengers turned pale. This Thok could be no other than Loki in the shape of a woman.

At the news that Loki alone prevented Balder's return, the gods and goddesses were filled with a vast anger. The ground shook with it, the oceans roared, the heavens thundered. Even Frigga was past weeping.

One thing was clear. Loki must be found and punished.

But Loki, fearing the wrath of the Aesir, fled to a mountain far from Asgard. There he built himself a small house with four doors. From it he could look out in all directions—north, east, south, and west. No enemy could surprise him.

Yet Loki was never at ease. Often, during the day, he took the shape of a salmon and hid in a pool in the river, behind a waterfall. But not even this made him feel secure, for the anger of the Aesir had no bounds, and Loki knew it.

Still hoping to outwit them, he tried to picture how the gods might try to capture him when they came, as come they would. Sitting before his fire, Loki twisted some linen twine into loops, then meshed these together. As he worked, his eyes darted from door to door.

Suddenly he saw in the distance, coming over a hill, a whole company of the Aesir. Throwing his handiwork into the fire, Loki dashed from his hut and into the river, changing his shape as he plunged.

When the Aesir arrived, the first one to enter Loki's hut was Kvasir, famous for wisdom and inspiration. On the hearth, in the form of hot, white ashes, Kvasir saw an object that could be used to catch a fish. Inspired still further, Kvasir predicted, "As a fish and with a contraption like that Loki will be captured."

So, taking the outline in the ashes as their model, the Aesir fashioned the device they needed. Nets have been made this way ever since.

At the river, they cast their net into the pool at the base of the waterfall. Then, with Thor on one bank and the rest of the Aesir on the other, they dragged the river bottom.

Loki, in his salmon form, shot ahead of them, then hid among some rocks at the bottom of the river. So, retracing their steps, the gods cast their net again.

Loki swam swiftly downstream and, when the gods drew near, sprang from the water, over the net, and back upstream, a gold and silver shape slithering through the clear water.

Again and again the Aesir tried to catch him. Finally Thor waded out to the middle of the river and, when Loki the salmon tried to leap over the net, Thor grasped him. Even then, he nearly escaped, the slippery salmon sliding through Thor's fingers, all the way to its tail. But Thor held it securely, squeezing with all his might, and to this day a salmon's body tapers toward the tail.

"Loki's last evil deed has been done," pronounced the Aesir. But to be sure of this, they put him in a cave, chained to a rock. Above his head they placed a poisonous serpent, hung so that the venom would drip onto Loki's face.

Loki's wife Sigyn stationed herself beside him, holding a cup to catch the venom. Only when Sigyn left to empty the cup did any poison reach Loki's face. Each time that happened, Loki shuddered so violently that the ground shook with what is now called an earthquake.

There, in this cave, Loki, son of darkness, cold, and evil, is doomed to remain until the final battle of the gods and the Frost Giants, and the world's end.

But what of Balder? Is he doomed to remain in Hel? Only until the final battle and the world's end. But before the battle will come the Terrible Winter—three winters in one with no summers in between. Winds colder and fiercer than any ever known will sweep down from the North. Living things will be pierced to the quick.

The earth will be frightened and begin to tremble, toppling the World Tree. Mountains will crash down and seas rise to engulf the land. Giant wolves will devour the sun and moon.

Loki will break loose and sail with a shipload of Frost Giants to invade Asgard.

From burning regions to the south, the Fire Giant Surt will ride forth to join forces with the Frost Giants. Then, after the final battle, Surt will wave his flaming sword, and the worlds will be consumed by fire.

But this will not be the end. Later, the earth will rise from the seas, fresh and green again. And hidden in a wood, nourished on dew, will be two mortals, Lif and Lifthrasir. From them will come others to repeople the earth. The sun will have a daughter who will travel the heavens, outshining her mother.

Then, and only then, from the cold, dark regions beneath the worlds, Balder the Bright will rise again, as radiant and kindly as before.

For this is what Odin whispered to Balder on his funeral pyre: that just as spring returns after the death of winter, so Balder would return, and life would go on.

59

AUTHOR'S NOTE

For centuries, Norse, Celtic, and Germanic people of Europe held special rites marking Balder's death and return to life. The summer solstice or Midsummer, the longest day of the year, they thought of as the time of Balder's death, for after that the days grew shorter. On Midsummer Eve, they gathered mistletoe in Balder's honor and burned balefires to light his way to the underworld.

At the winter solstice or Midwinter, the shortest day of the year, these people celebrated Balder's return. They knew that from then on the days would become longer and the sun stronger, riding higher in the sky. Once again they gathered mistletoe in honor of Balder, and to illumine his return to the heavens, they burned yule logs.

In time, belief in such pagan gods gave way to the Christian religion, and the winter solstice festival was replaced by the celebration of Christmas. But the myth of Balder, with its power and beauty, refused to die. In many different versions, it was handed down in oral and then written form to the present day.

Over the centuries, the very mistletoe that had killed Balder found its way into Christmas. Kissing or being kissed under the mistletoe became a joyful part of the Christmas scene. Like holly and other evergreens, mistletoe had long been a symbol of everlasting life. The Druid priests of western Europe had cut it from their sacred oak at the winter solstice and exchanged kisses as part of the ceremony. Hoping to ward off evil spirits, people hung sprigs of mistletoe above their doorways; all who entered received a kiss as a token of friendship.

As regards Balder and the deadly mistletoe, storytellers of later Christian times were in a dilemma. In order to give the myth a prettier ending and to help explain a now popular Christmas custom, some storytellers changed the events in the myth or borrowed elements from it to concoct folktales.

In one such sentimental tale, after each of the Aesir in turn had tried in vain to bring Balder back to life, his mother Frigga finally succeeded. The tears she had shed for Balder became the tiny white, pearly, berries on the mistletoe plant. In her joy, Frigga decreed that never again would mistletoe harm anyone. Instead, each who passed beneath this plant would receive a kiss as a token of love.

My own version of the myth of Balder is patterned largely after portions of the 13th century Icelandic *Prose Edda* of Snorri Sturluson.

ABOUT THE AUTHOR

Edna Barth rediscovered the myth of *Balder and the Mistletoe* when she was doing research for her non-fiction book, *Holly, Reindeer, and Colored Lights: the Story of the Christmas Symbols*, and decided to retell it as an individual book.

Mrs. Barth is the author of many books on the Clarion list that have been well-received by both adult reviewers and young readers. Besides her book about Christmas symbols she has explored the meaning of the symbols of Easter, Thanksgiving, Halloween, Valentine's Day, and St. Patrick's Day in such titles as *Lilies, Rabbits, and Painted Eggs* and *Shamrocks, Harps, and Shillelaghs*. Her retellings of holiday stories include *Jack O'Lantern* for Halloween and *Cupid and Psyche* for Valentine's Day. She has also written a perceptive biography of Emily Dickinson, *I'm Nobody! Who Are You?*, aimed at 8–12-year-old readers and accompanied by a generous selection of Dickinson's poems.

A former editor-in-chief of children's books with a major publisher, Mrs. Barth lives in New York City and East Hampton, New York.

A TRIBUTE TO RICHARD CUFFARI

The illustrations for *Balder and the Mistletoe* were among the last Richard Cuffari was able to complete before his untimely death on October 10, 1978. The bold pictorial compositions, vivid character portrayals, and strong sense of drama in them epitomize the qualities Mr. Cuffari brought to the almost two hundred children's books he illustrated between 1968 and 1978.

An admirer of good writing, Mr. Cuffari concentrated on illustrating novels and longer non-fiction books, although he was well aware that the lion's share of critical attention went to the illustrators of picture books for young children. Still, he had the satisfaction of doing the pictures for books by some of today's finest writers for children and young people.

His work is bound to linger in the memories of the children who see it. And it will serve as a touchstone and inspiration for future artists who, like Richard Cuffari, want to devote their best efforts to book illustration.   *—James Giblin*